# Teddy Tales
## First day at school

BYEWAY
B O O K S

It's the start of the new term and Teddy arrives
at school with his friends. They are all
very excited.

"The new teacher is very pretty," says Pickle.

"Well I hope she is kind too," answers Tino.

Lily gasps, "Oh! I love her red dress."

"Come in," says the teacher, "but not all
at once!" she laughs.

"Can I sit next to you, Teddy?" asks Tino.

"I am Miss Kitty, and I will be your teacher for the whole year. I would like each one of you to stand up and introduce yourself to the rest of the class. So who would like to start?"

"Me," says Teddy, "I am called Teddy and I live in Highstone Forest."

Next, it's Lily's turn, followed by the others.

"Open your books," instructs Miss Kitty,
"and write your name at the top of the page."
"Where is my pencil?" asks Pickle anxiously,
"I had it this morning."
"Over here," cries Teddy, waving a pencil.
"I found it on the path, your bag must have
been open."
"Thank you," says Pickle, sticking his tongue
out at Lily who is laughing at him.

The bell rings for lunch break. The friends
unwrap their packed lunches.
Meanwhile, poor Pickle searches desperately
for his carrots.
"I also found these on the path!" laughs Teddy
as he hands over Pickle's bag of carrots.
"Thank you," mumbles Pickle happily, with
a mouthful of carrot.
The friends enjoy their lunch.

"Hey! Do you want to play hopscotch?"
asks Lily.

"No, that's a girl's game!" shouts Tino.

"Hurry up Pig Pig, we need you in goal,"
calls Teddy.

"Don't wait for me," Pig Pig yells over his
shoulder, "I need to go to the toilet!"

After lunch, they do some painting.

"What have you painted Teddy?"

asks Miss Kitty. "Is it a monster?"

"No...um... it's supposed to be you Miss Kitty,

but it hasn't worked out as I meant it to!"

Tino laughs so much, that he spills his

paint over Teddy's picture.

"I'm so sorry Teddy!" gasps Tino.

"It doesn't matter Tino, it wasn't very good

anyway," Teddy reassures him.

"Well, you have all been very good on your first day so I have prepared a puppet show for you," announces Miss Kitty.

"Yippee!" "Hooray!" "Oh! Miss, thank you!" Joyful sounds echo around the classroom.

"Once upon a time, a little girl was going to see her grandmother, when she met a nasty big wolf...," Miss Kitty reads from behind the puppet theatre.

"I don't like wolves," whimpers Pickle.

The animals enjoy the puppet show and when
it ends, they thank Miss Kitty.
School is finished for today.
Pickle is a bit worried by the story of the wolf
but Teddy and Tino look after him as they head
off home to Highstone Forest.